SKYLARK CHOOSE YOUR OWN ADVENTURE® · 16

"I DON'T LIKE CHOOSE YOUR OWN ADVENTURE® BOOKS. I *LOVE* THEM!" says Jessica Gordon, age 10. And now kids between the ages of six and nine can choose their own adventures too. Here's what kids have to say about the Skylark Choose Your Own Adventure® books.

"These are my favorite books because you can pick whatever choice you want— and the story is all about you."
—**Katy Alson,** *age 8*

"I love finding out how my story will end."
—**Joss Williams,** *age 9*

"I like all the illustrations!"
—**Savitri Brightfield,** *age 7*

"A six-year-old friend and I have lots of fun making the decisions together."
—**Peggy Marcus** *(adult)*

Bantam Skylark Books in the Choose Your Own
  Adventure® Series
Ask your bookseller for the books you have missed

 #1 THE CIRCUS

 #2 THE HAUNTED HOUSE

 #3 SUNKEN TREASURE

 #4 YOUR VERY OWN ROBOT

 #5 GORGA, THE SPACE MONSTER

 #6 THE GREEN SLIME

 #7 HELP! YOU'RE SHRINKING

 #8 INDIAN TRAIL

 #9 DREAM TRIPS

#10 THE GENIE IN THE BOTTLE

#11 THE BIGFOOT MYSTERY

#12 THE CREATURE FROM MILLER'S POND

#13 JUNGLE SAFARI

#14 THE SEARCH FOR CHAMP

#15 THE THREE WISHES

#16 DRAGONS!

DRAGONS!

JIM RAZZI

ILLUSTRATED BY KEVIN CALLAHAN

An R. A. Montgomery Book

A BANTAM SKYLARK BOOK®
TORONTO · NEW YORK · LONDON · SYDNEY

RL 2, 007–009

DRAGONS!

A Bantam Skylark Book / April 1984

CHOOSE YOUR OWN ADVENTURE® is a registered
trademark of Bantam Books, Inc.

Original conception of Edward Packard

Skylark Books is a registered trademark of
Bantam Books, Inc.
Registered in U.S. Patent and Trademark Office
and elsewhere.

Front cover art by Paul Granger.

ISBN 0-553-15242-4

Published simultaneously in the United States and Canada

Bantam Books are published by Bantam Books, Inc. Its
trademark, consisting of the words "Bantam Books" and the
portrayal of a rooster, is Registered in U.S. Patent and Trademark Office and in other countries. Marca Registrada. Bantam Books, Inc., 666 Fifth Avenue, New York, New York 10103.

PRINTED IN THE UNITED STATES OF AMERICA

CW 0 9 8 7 6 5 4 3 2 1

DRAGONS!

READ THIS FIRST!!!

Most books are about other people.

This book is about you—and your quest for dragons.

What happens to you depends on what you decide to do.

Do not read this book from the first page through to the last page.

Instead, start at page one and read until you come to your first choice. Decide what you want to do. Then turn to the page shown and see what happens.

When you come to the end of a story, go back and try another choice. Every choice leads to a new adventure.

If you find a dragon's treasure, you could be rich—but not if a dragon finds *you* first!

Good luck!

You're back in olden times in the days of **1** bold knights, fair maidens, and fierce dragons!

You and your parents live in a huge castle. Your father is a poor but brave knight who does many good deeds. In fact, he is going off to do a good deed at this very moment. You ask your father if you can go with him.

"I'm sorry. You're too young," he says firmly as he rides off.

You walk away glumly. It's going to be very boring staying at home.

You decide to pass some time exploring the castle. Soon you find yourself in a tower where you have never been before. Suddenly your eye catches something on the floor—an old book covered with dust. It's all about dragons!

Turn to page 3.

The book is really interesting. You learn that dragons can breathe out fire and smoke. Some can fly, talk, and even perform magic. And sometimes they guard fabulous treasures. The book warns you to be careful of dragons, though, since they are often evil and bad-tempered.

You are very excited. You'd love to find a dragon's treasure so that your family wouldn't be poor anymore. Suddenly you have a great idea. You will go off on your own to look for dragons!

Quickly you put on the suit of armor that you got for your birthday. It fits perfectly. You feel like a real knight.

You step outdoors into the sunshine. Outside the castle you see a huge, dark forest and a deep, green valley. Should you go through the forest or down into the valley?

If you go through the forest, turn to page 6.

*If you go down into the valley,
turn to page 5.*

You take a path that leads down into the valley. When you get there, a strange silence greets you. The air is very still—there aren't even any birds singing. Where are all the animals?

You are still wondering about this when a huge shadow passes over you. You look up, and your heart skips a beat. Now you know why all the animals are gone. A monstrous green dragon is flying overhead. It sees *you* and spirals down.

Quickly you look around. You see a big hole at the foot of a hill. Should you face the dragon or jump into the hole?

If you face the dragon, turn to page 8.

If you jump into the hole, turn to page 10.

You head for the dark forest. It seems a likely place to find dragons. You take a path that leads deep into the woods.

Twisted black trees grow along the path. Their branches clutch at you like grasping

claws as you pass. Strange whispers echo
through the woods. You tell yourself, "It's just
the wind."

Turn to page 12.

8   You decide to face the dragon. You watch as the huge creature glides to a landing a few feet away.

"Greetings, small knight!" hisses the dragon.

"Gr—greetings," you stammer. Then you realize that the dragon is talking.

"You can talk!" you say. "I've read about that."

"Really?" asks the dragon in a soothing voice. "Did you also read that we can perform magic?"

"Why, yes, I did," you answer excitedly. "What can you do?"

"Well, let's see," says the dragon, looking you over. "I can change you into a bird. Then you could fly like me."

If you would like to be changed into a bird, turn to page 16.

If you would rather stay as you are, turn to page 24.

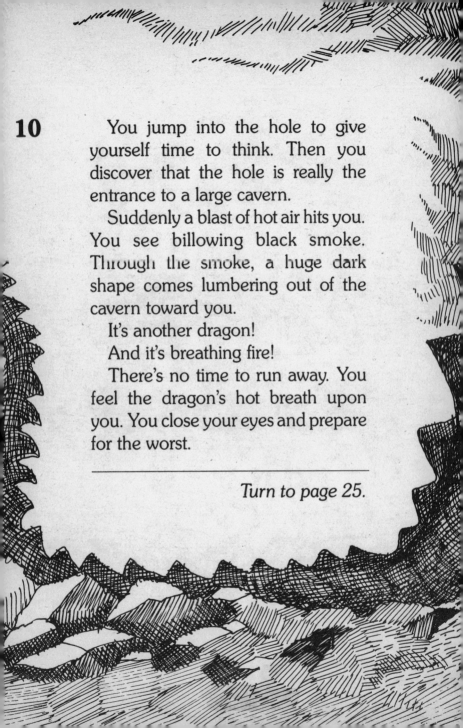

10   You jump into the hole to give yourself time to think. Then you discover that the hole is really the entrance to a large cavern.

Suddenly a blast of hot air hits you. You see billowing black smoke. Through the smoke, a huge dark shape comes lumbering out of the cavern toward you.

It's another dragon!

And it's breathing fire!

There's no time to run away. You feel the dragon's hot breath upon you. You close your eyes and prepare for the worst.

Turn to page 25.

12   You are having second thoughts about looking for dragons in this forest.

    Suddenly you hear the sound of crunching footsteps.

    They're coming from behind a huge rock. It might be a wild beast, or it might be . . . a dragon!

    You're not sure you want to know.

    Maybe you should make a run for it.

*If you look behind the rock,
turn to page 20.*

If you make a run for it, turn to page 14.

You are alone again in the dark forest. You **13** wonder if you're going to meet any more dragons. You still dream of finding one that's guarding treasure. You decide to continue your search.

Deeper and deeper into the forest you go. . . .

It is getting dark now.

You are weary and lost. You want to return home. Your mother will be worried, and besides, your feet hurt. But you don't know which way is home.

You find another path. You hope it will lead out of the forest.

You walk along the path, peering ahead for signs of danger.

Then you come to a sharp bend in the path that winds around a huge hill.

If you walk around the bend, turn to page 21.

If you climb over the hill, turn to page 29.

14   You take off down the path. You stumble through the forest as fast as you can.

All of a sudden, you trip over something on the ground. You look down and see a baby dragon!

The little dragon's leg is caught in a cruel-looking iron trap. You wonder if you should try to open it on your own. But you might hurt the little dragon even more if you did it wrong.

If you open the trap, turn to page 18.

If you don't open it, turn to page 36.

16   It might be interesting to be a bird. "All right," you say. "Change me into a bird."

The dragon says some magic words and suddenly . . . Poof!

You're a bird!

You flap your wings and start to fly. From high in the sky, you look down. Everything seems so tiny! Then you see the dragon flying after you. It comes very close, staring at you with large yellow eyes.

"I never did like to eat humans," it tells you. "Birds are my favorite dish. Most of them are

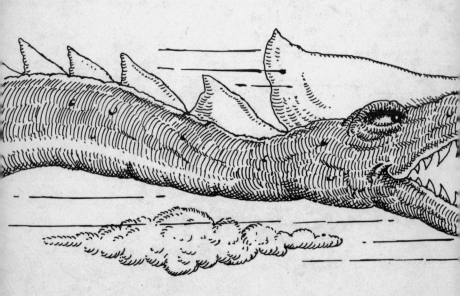

too fast for me, but you're just right. You're big and fat and slow!"

Now you realize what's happening. You try to scream, but all that comes out is: "Squawk! Squawk!"

The dragon opens its huge mouth and flies closer. Its teeth gleam in the sunlight. You realize too late that you've been tricked into becoming a dragon's lunch!

The End

18   The young dragon seems to be in great pain. You decide that you have nothing to lose by trying to open the trap. Using a big stick of wood as a lever, you pry open the trap.

After you free the dragon, it licks you with a long, slippery tongue.

"Thank you for helping me," it says. "I won't forget your good deed." You are about to answer when you notice a strange thing. The little dragon is growing!

The dragon notices your surprise and explains: "Dragons grow up in less than a day. I was born this morning—and by tonight, I'll be full-grown."

"Gadzooks!" you say. "That's amazing!"

You are about to ask the dragon more when it scampers off.

"Wait!" you call. But it's too late. The dragon has disappeared into the thick woods.

Turn to page 13.

20 You decide to be brave and look behind the rock. Slowly you walk up to it. You can hear heavy breathing.

Your knees are shaking in spite of yourself. You tiptoe closer. . . .

Suddenly something jumps at you from behind the rock. It knocks you down before you can see what it is.

You look up fearfully.

Turn to page 45.

You take the path around the bend. You're **21**
halfway around the curve when the ground
suddenly gives way. You fall into a big hole.

It's a trap!

You look around quickly for ways to
escape.

Suddenly you hear thunderous footsteps.
BOOM! BOOM! BOOM!

Something is coming to see what it has
caught.

Go on to the next page.

The footsteps sound closer and closer. Then they stop. You look up fearfully.

Slowly an ugly, scaly head appears at the opening of the hole. Yellow eyes glare down at you angrily.

It's another dragon! You're doomed!

Turn to page 30.

24 You also remember that you're afraid of heights.

"No," you say, "I don't think I want to be a bird. I like myself the way I am."

"So do I," says the dragon with a strange look. Suddenly it says: "I would like to show you some magic, but—"

"But what?" you ask.

Turn to page 26.

Suddenly you hear singing. You open your eyes.

It's the dragon!

It stops singing and looks at you.

"I'm so glad you came to my cavern," it hisses. "It's about time someone heard my wonderful voice."

Turn to page 33.

26   "You'll have to kiss me first," the dragon answers.

"KISS YOU!" you exclaim. "Why?"

"I can't tell you why," answers the dragon. "Just do as I say."

If you decide to kiss the dragon, turn to page 42.

If you decide not to kiss the dragon, turn to page 38.

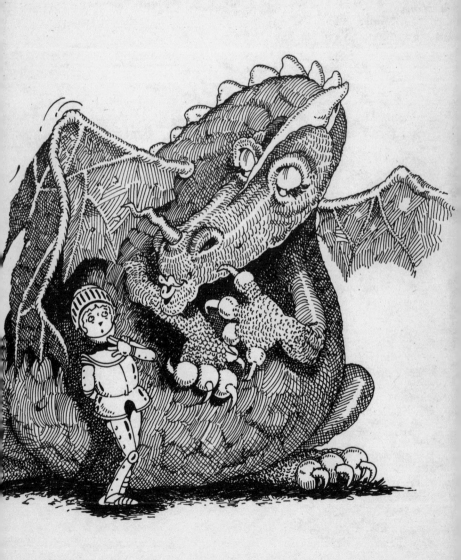

You climb up the hill. As you reach the top, you stop dead in your tracks. The hill levels onto a rise of land. In front of you stands a black castle. It looks evil and bleak. You wonder who lives there.

As you move closer, you can see a coat of arms carved above the doorway. It shows a huge and terrible dragon.

You don't like the looks of the castle, but you need shelter for the night.

Should you go in, or take your chances in the forest?

If you enter the castle, turn to page 35.

If you go back into the forest, turn to page 46.

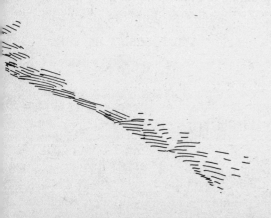

30   You think it's the end when suddenly the dragon speaks.

"I'm very hungry," it hisses, "but my honor won't let me eat you."

You don't understand what the dragon is talking about.

"Don't you recognize me?" the dragon asks.

"N-no," you stammer. "Should I?"

"You released me from a trap today. I must repay you for your kindness," the dragon continues.

You let out a sigh of relief.

"I'm full-grown now, and I can fly. I'll take you wherever you want to go," says the dragon.

You say you want to go home. The dragon nods and lowers a scaly leg into the hole. You grab the leg and pull yourself up. Then you sit on the dragon's back as it slowly rises above the forest. You can see your castle in the distance.

You smile. It pays to do good deeds.

The End

The truth is that the dragon has a *terrible* **33** voice. But you don't dare tell it that. It might get mad at you and fry you on the spot. The dragon asks if you'd like to hear it sing some more.

"Uh, with pleasure," you say.

"Good," answers the dragon with a satisfied grin. "I can sing for *hours.*"

Oh, no! You groan as you sit down on a rock. You were preparing for the worst, and it seems as if you got it!

The End

You decide to go into the black castle for **35** the night. Slowly you walk through the doorway. The place looks deserted and very old. Cobwebs hang everywhere, and the walls are slick with slime. Your only light is the moonlight streaming through the windows.

Your footsteps echo on the stone floor.

At last you come to a great hall. To your surprise, torches are burning along the walls. What's going on?

At the end of the hall you see two huge doors. One is green, the other purple. You wonder where they lead.

All of a sudden, you trip over a stone slab. It has writing on it.

Turn to page 44.

36   You decide not to try to open the trap. Meanwhile, the young dragon is squealing in pain.

Just then you hear a terrible roar. A huge dragon breaks through the trees. It's the young dragon's mother! She thinks you've hurt her baby.

Oh, no! How can you explain that you didn't mean any harm?

It seems that you can't.

The dragon charges at you, breathing fire and smoke. There is no escape.

The End

38   You look at the dragon. "I—I can't," you say.

"Why not?" asks the dragon.

You decide to tell the truth. "You're too ugly," you blurt out.

At that, the dragon rears up and shoots flames and smoke out of its nostrils. You've gotten it mad! It paws the ground.

You realize that you can't win in a face-to-face fight with this gigantic creature. You look around. There's a forest behind you where you could hide. You wait for your chance and then head for the woods.

The dragon lumbers after you, but on the ground it's much too slow. You plunge into the woods and keep on running.

Deep in the forest you come to a path by a lake with tall reeds. Should you take the path or hide there in the reeds?

If you take the path, turn to page 52.

If you hide in the reeds, turn to page 41.

You decide to hide in the reeds. You're sure the dragon won't see you there. Suddenly you hear a sound coming from the lake. You turn around. You can't believe your eyes!

A beautiful lady is rising out of the water!

In her hand she holds a golden sword. She walks right up to you and offers you the sword.

"Young knight," she says, "I am the lady of the lake. With this magic sword you can protect yourself from any dragon."

"Why are you giving it to me?" you ask.

"Because your heart is brave and good," she answers.

Turn to page 54.

42   Kissing a dragon is the strangest thing you've ever been asked to do. But you're really curious about what magic the dragon can perform. You decide to kiss it.

The dragon lowers its big scaly head.

You gulp once and kiss it quickly.

Whooomp! . . . POOF!

The dragon is gone. In its place stands a beautiful princess!

"You have released me from an evil spell," she says softly. "A witch cast a spell on me and

turned me into a dragon. Only if a knight kissed me without knowing why could the curse be broken."

"On my honor," you say, "I'm glad I decided to kiss you."

The princess smiles and takes your hand. You smile back. How lucky you are! You went looking for treasure and you found a friend. That's worth much, much more.

The End

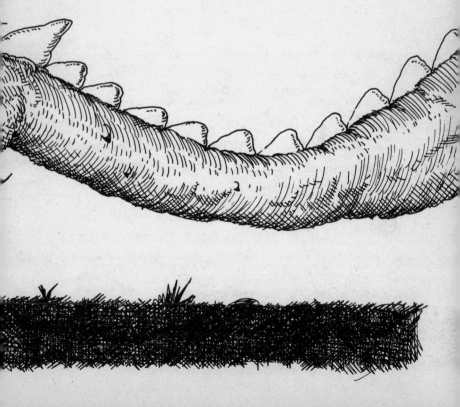

44

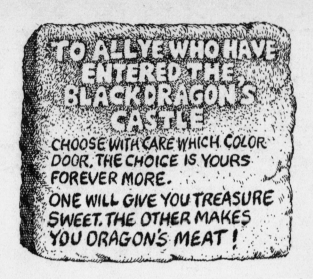

TO ALL YE WHO HAVE ENTERED THE BLACK DRAGON'S CASTLE

CHOOSE WITH CARE WHICH COLOR DOOR. THE CHOICE IS YOURS FOREVER MORE.

ONE WILL GIVE YOU TREASURE SWEET. THE OTHER MAKES YOU DRAGON'S MEAT!

If you choose the right door, you'll find treasure. If you choose the wrong door, you'll find the black dragon!

You face the two doors. You have never had such a tough choice to make in your life. On your knight's honor, the door you choose will be final. You cannot choose again.

Which door will you open?

If you choose the green door, turn to page 49.

If you choose the purple door, turn to page 51.

It's a very tall knight!

He looks dangerous, but you notice something familiar about his armor.

"Father!" you shout.

Your father raises his visor and smiles.

"What are you doing here?" he asks. "I thought you were a wild beast."

"What are *you* doing here?" you answer. "I thought you were a dragon!"

"Why, as far as I know, there haven't been dragons around here for years!" laughs your father.

You tell him about the book that described dragons and treasure. "I thought we'd be rich," you say sadly.

"Doing good deeds is reward enough for me," your father answers. "I just saved a king from a wild boar." He grins and holds up a bag of gold. "He gave me this as a reward."

Your father puts his arm around you. "Now let's go home and hear no more of dragons," he says.

You look back at the forest.

"Too bad there aren't dragons anymore," you say. "I would have liked to meet one."

The End

46   You decide that any place would be better than the black castle. So you turn off the hill and stumble back into the forest. You walk and walk until your legs ache.

At first you're scared, but then you become braver. You gather some wood to make a fire. You start rubbing two sticks together as your father taught you. Soon you have a cheery fire going. You settle down as best you can.

You look up and see the stars twinkling through the trees.

Ah, well, you think, a little *knight* in the forest shouldn't be afraid of a little *night* in the forest.

The End

You choose the green door. You walk up to it nervously. Before you open it, you listen, but you can't hear a thing. The door is too thick.

"Well," you say aloud, "it's now or never!"

You grasp the iron latch and swing the door open.

Darkness!

You walk inside the chamber. . . .

The door slams shut behind you.

You're trapped!

Then you see a flicker of light. It's coming from a room around the corner.

Suddenly you hear a loud hissing.

Then you see a scaly head coming around the corner.

"Oh, no!" you yell. "The black dragon!"

The End

You choose the purple door. You walk up to it nervously. Before you open it, you listen, but you can't hear a thing. The door is too thick.

"Well," you say aloud, "it's now or never!"

You grasp the iron latch and swing the door open.

Darkness!

You walk inside the chamber. . . .

Suddenly the door slams shut behind you.

You're trapped!

Then you see a flicker of light. It's coming from a room around the bend. You walk ahead slowly and turn the corner.

TREASURE!

The room is piled high with gold and silver and jewels!

You chose the right door! You and your parents will be rich!

The End

52 You take the path.

It winds its way through the forest and then suddenly comes out on a dusty road. Where are you?

Then you hear music. You see a horse-drawn cart coming slowly down the road. On the cart are a band of minstrels playing flutes, guitars, and little drums.

You stand in the middle of the road and wave your arms. "Stop! Please stop!" you shout.

Surprised, the minstrels stop the cart and their music.

"I am tired," you say. "Will you let me ride with you?"

"Of course, young knight!" they answer.

When you climb up into the cart, you ask where they're going. To your surprise, you find that they are going to *your* castle to play music for your parents!

You lean back in the cart with a sigh. It's going to be a long time before you hunt dragons again.

The End

54   You blush as you take the sword. You are about to say more when you hear a terrible hiss. It's the dragon! It's found you!

The lady of the lake smiles at you.

"Don't be afraid," she says. Then she disappears.

You're not afraid. You turn to face the dragon with your magic sword—and you know you'll win!

The End

ABOUT THE AUTHOR

James Razzi is the bestselling author of numerous game, puzzle, and story books, including the Sherluck Bones Mystery-Detective and Slimy series, and *The Genie in the Bottle,* in the Bantam Skylark Choose Your Own Adventure series. Well over two and a half million copies of his books have been sold in the United States, Britain, and Canada. One, *The Star Trek Puzzle Manual,* was on the *New York Times* bestseller list for a number of weeks. His book *Don't Open This Box!* was picked as one of the "Books of the Year" by the Child Study Association.

ABOUT THE ILLUSTRATOR

Kevin Callahan has been an illustrator for fifteen years. In addition to illustrating children's books and textbooks, including *The Genie in the Bottle* in the Bantam Skylark Choose Your Own Adventure series, he has worked in advertising. He is also the creator of a syndicated comic strip and the author of a book on antiques. His work has received awards from the Society of Illustrators and the Art Directors' Club. Mr. Callahan lives in Norwalk, Connecticut.

Now you can have your favorite Choose Your Own Adventure® Series in a variety of sizes. Along with the popular pocket size, Bantam has introduced the Choose Your Own Adventure® series in a Skylark edition and also in Hardcover.

Now not only do you get to decide on how you want your adventures to end, you also get to decide on what size you'd like to collect them in.

SKYLARK EDITIONS

☐	15238	The Circus #1 E. Packard	$1.95
☐	15207	The Haunted House #2 R. A. Montgomery	$1.95
☐	15208	Sunken Treasure #3 E. Packard	$1.95
☐	15233	Your Very Own Robot #4 R. A. Montgomery	$1.96
☐	15308	Gorga, The Space Monster #5 E. Packard	$1.95
☐	15309	The Green Slime #6 S. Saunders	$1.95
☐	15195	Help! You're Shrinking #5 E. Packard	$1.95
☐	15201	Indian Trail #8 R. A. Montgomery	$1.95
☐	15191	The Genie In the Bottle #10 J. Razzi	$1.95
☐	15222	The Big Foot Mystery #11 L. Sonberg	$1.95
☐	15223	The Creature From Millers Pond #12 S. Saunders	$1.95
☐	15226	Jungle Safari #13 E. Packard	$1.95
☐	15227	The Search For Champ #14 S. Gilligan	$1.95

HARDCOVER EDITIONS

☐	05018	Sunken Treasure E. Packard	$6.95
☐	05019	Your Very Own Robot R. A. Montgomery	$6.95
☐	05031	Gorga, The Space Monster #5 E. Packard	$7.95
☐	05032	Green Slime #6 S. Saunders	$7.95

Prices and availability subject to change without notice.

Buy them at your local bookstore or use this handy coupon for ordering: